Welcome to...

# THE MAMMOTH
# ACADEMY

OSCAR WAS

A WOOLLY MAMMOTH.

AND SO WAS
ARABELLA.

# SOME OF THE OTHER

# PUPILS AT

# THE

# MAMMOTH ACADEMY

← FLY LIVED IN THE ACADEMY BUT WASN'T A ~~PUPIL~~ PUPIL.

CAVE CAT

ORMSBY

OWL

PRUNELLA

FOX

A FEW MORE *PUPILS OF*

# THE MAMMOTH ACADEMY

RHONDA

REGINALD

ROGER

REMI

REX

RUFUS

REENIE

GIANT
GROUND
SLOTH

CAVE
BEAR

# For Anne McNeil

# CHAPTER 1
# WELCOME TO THE ACADEMY

Oscar was a Woolly Mammoth, and so was Arabella. They lived a long time ago in the Ice Age.

They used to spend their time playing in the snowfields, exploring caves, making ice sculptures, and doing all the other things that young mammoths like to do. But of course there always comes a point in a young mammoth's life when it's time to grow up a little bit and start school.

Oscar wasn't looking forward to it. He didn't like the idea of being cooped up in a classroom and told what to do. Arabella, on the other hand, was really excited. She loved the idea of learning new things and making new friends.

One day a Very Important Letter arrived –
by mammoth mail of course.

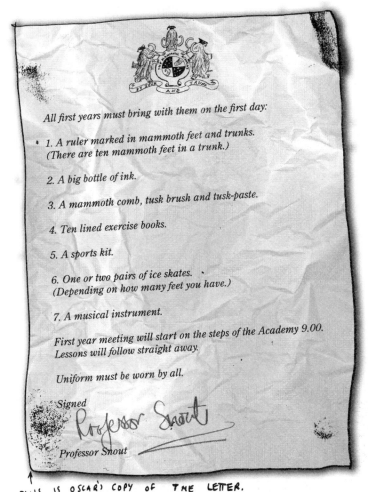

All first years must bring with them on the first day:

1. A ruler marked in mammoth feet and trunks.
(There are ten mammoth feet in a trunk.)

2. A big bottle of ink.

3. A mammoth comb, tusk brush and tusk-paste.

4. Ten lined exercise books.

5. A sports kit.

6. One or two pairs of ice skates.
(Depending on how many feet you have.)

7. A musical instrument.

First year meeting will start on the steps of the Academy 9.00.
Lessons will follow straight away.

Uniform must be worn by all.

Signed

*Professor Snout*

THIS IS OSCAR'S COPY OF THE LETTER.
ARABELLA PUT HERS NEATLY AWAY SOME WHERE.
OSCAR SHOVED HIS UNDER HIS HAT.

That first morning was cold and crisp, and very snowy, as the animals left their homes to begin the journey across the icy wastes to the Academy.

There was a friendly megaloceros to help them across the glacier, and signs to make sure they didn't stray over the cliff into the marsh.

It seemed to take a long time to reach the Academy, especially with Oscar dragging his big feet, but eventually they arrived at the gates.

Inside was a noisy throng of animals of all shapes and sizes. Oscar and Arabella recognized a few of the faces, but most of them they had never seen before.

Suddenly a gong rang out.

On the steps stood
the headmistress. She was
quite a stern looking mammoth,
not at all like the old auntie mammoths back
at the herd. But when she smiled her eyes
twinkled.

BONG! BONG! BONG! BONG!

'Welcome,' she said. 'Here are your maps and
timetables. Off you go …'

And that was it. Oscar and Arabella's new
school life had begun.

The West Wing

Professor Bristle's Classroom

Concert Hall

More Classrooms

HERE IS ALABELLA' COPY OF THE MAP. AS YOU CAN

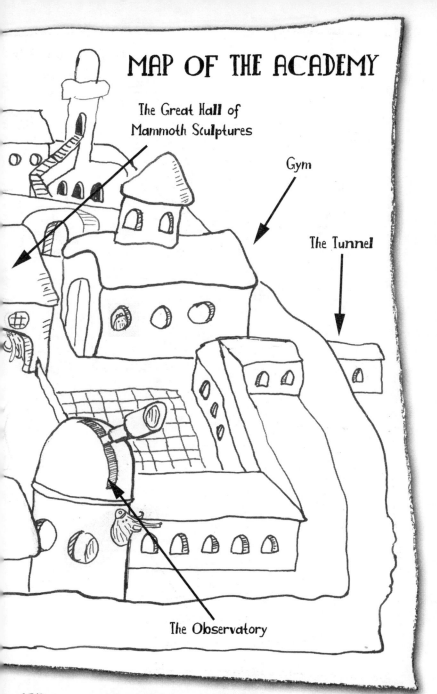

# MAP OF THE ACADEMY

The Great Hall of
Mammoth Sculptures

Gym

The Tunnel

The Observatory

SEE SHE HAS KEPT IT NEAT AND TIDY.

t Wing

Professor Bristle's
Classroom

Concert
Hall

More Classrooms

↑ THIS IS OSCAR'S COPY OF THE MAP.

(I THINK HIS BOTTLE OF INK MIGHT HAVE LEAKED IN HIS BAG.)

# CHAPTER 2
# FIRST LESSONS

HUMPH!

Oscar's first lesson at the Academy did not go terribly well. To begin with he was late. Somewhere in the East Wing he had ended up having a disagreement with Arabella over the best way of finding Professor Bristle's classroom.

Oscar had insisted he knew exactly where he was going. Arabella had insisted that Oscar had the map upside down and that he had better follow her if he wanted any hope of arriving on time.

Having decided to strike out on his own,
Oscar found lots of interesting things to look at …

... before finally coming across the MYSTERIOUS TRACKS.

Now – if you saw the MYSTERIOUS TRACKS what would you do? Oscar decided to follow them (of course!).

They were quite faint due to the heavy snow-fall of the day and disappeared altogether in places, but in addition to the tracks there were little bits of orange peel that were easier to spot.

Eventually the trail led him to a big warm room that smelt of baked cakes and cabbage.

'Hey you! What are you doing here?' shouted a scary looking mammoth. Twice as wide as she was tall, she wore an apron and a big hat and was dusted with flour. She was waving a rolling pin in her trunk.

'I hope you're not the young scamp who's been stealing oranges from the larder.'

'Errrrr … um,' mumbled Oscar.

'Nothing to say for yourself, eh … ?'

The big mammoth in the apron plonked the rolling pin down and deftly picked Oscar up by the scruff of his neck.

'Right, you're coming with me … !'

And so Oscar arrived at Professor Bristle's class – late, covered in flour, and with Cook accusing him of stealing oranges. All the time he was trying to explain about the MYSTERIOUS TRACKS and the orange peel … but not getting anywhere.

'I can assure you that I shall get to the bottom of all this …' was all Cook said.

Professor Bristle didn't seem too interested in what Oscar had to say either. He merely told Oscar to dust himself off, take a seat and apply himself to investigating the mathematical problem of $1+1=$ as written on the blackboard.

The only seat left in the class was next to a fox that Oscar didn't know. Across the classroom Arabella was sitting next to Ormsby, the woolly rhino. He seemed to be having a good chuckle about Oscar's scruffy state. The rabbits seemed to think it was quite funny, too.

'Don't worry,' said Fox. 'I'll help you catch up – and what's all this about MYSTERIOUS TRACKS? It sounds terribly exciting!'

And although he had never met Fox before, Oscar immediately felt like he had found a friend.

# CHAPTER 3
# MORE LESSONS AND JOKES

After that, Oscar's first day seemed to go a little more smoothly. They had lessons of:

Geography, which was interesting.

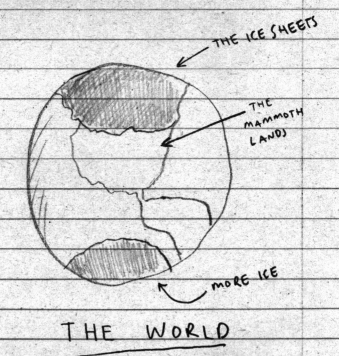

THE ICE SHEETS

THE MAMMOTH LANDS

MORE ICE

THE WORLD

# A GLACIER

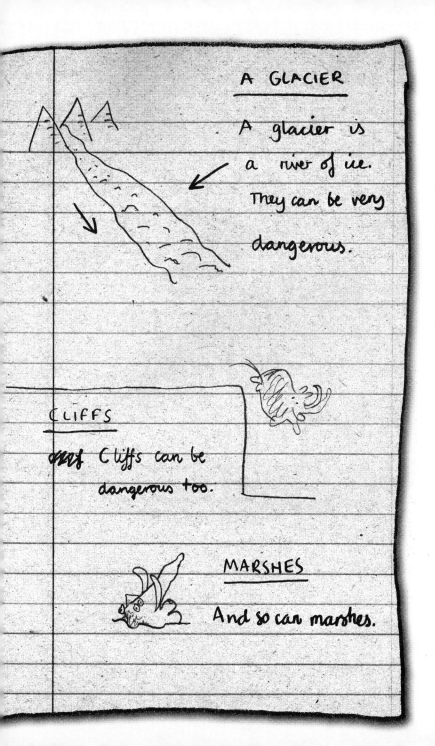

A glacier is a river of ice. They can be very dangerous.

## CLIFFS

Cliffs can be dangerous too.

## MARSHES

And so can marshes.

Skiing, which Arabella enjoyed.

And Music.

Oscar and Fox particularly enjoyed the music lesson.

Until eventually,
BONG BONG BONG BONG!
it was time to go home …

On the way home Oscar introduced Arabella to Fox and Arabella introduced Oscar to Prunella.

As they walked, Prunella talked about all the problems of being a small mammal in the Ice Age and which of the rodents she thought was cutest at school. Arabella thought Prunella was great.

And Fox told them lots of jokes that Oscar
found hilarious.

'What's the difference between a Woolly
Mammoth and a gooseberry?

*Woolly Mammoths don't grow on bushes!*'

'**What's the difference between a
Woolly Mammoth and an orange?**

*You can't comb an orange!*'

'**What's the difference between a
Woolly Mammoth and a strawberry?**

*A strawberry is bright red!*'

'**What's the difference between a Woolly
Mammoth and a currant bun?**

*A currant bun doesn't weigh two tons!*'

44

'**W**hy did the Woolly Mammoth sit on the orange?

*He wanted to play squash!*'

'**C**an a Woolly Mammoth jump higher than a mountain?

*Yes, mountains can't jump!*'

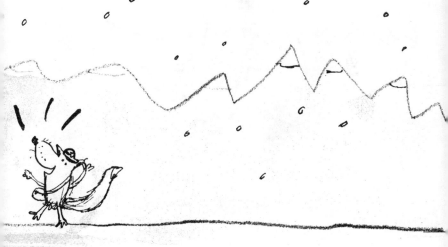

'Goodbye! See you all tomorrow!'

# CHAPTER 4
## OSCAR'S THEORY AND FOX'S GREAT IDEA

The next morning at the Academy there was a special assembly called for all the staff and students.

It seemed that in the summer holiday, when the Academy was closed, somebody had broken into Cook's kitchen and stolen nearly the entire year's stock of oranges.

This was very shocking news indeed, as I'm sure you are aware that mammoths are very fond of oranges, and they are good for them too. Mammoths like oranges probably as much as you like chips and chocolate!

The headmistress made it clear that if anyone knew anything about the orange theft, they ought to tell a teacher immediately.

After that things became a little difficult for Oscar. Teachers would sit him up the front of the class and give him the 'I've got my eye on you so don't try anything' look.

And if Arabella, Prunella or Fox introduced

him to any of their friends it would be as, 'Oscar, you
know the one that got caught by Cook with the
oranges,' because news at school travels fast – of
course.

Fox had heard some new jokes too.

'**H**ow did the strawberry thief get found out?
*He got caught red handed!*'

'**W**hy did the orange thief get away?
*Well, you can't catch someone orange handed can
you!*'

'**W**hy did the Woolly Mammoth sit on the
orange?

*He didn't want it stolen!*'

But all joking aside, Oscar thought the situation was a serious one and he had decided that he ought to be the one to solve it.

That evening on the way home Oscar was quiet and thoughtful. Professor Bristle's lessons on sums had got him thinking.

$$1 + 1 = 2$$

The strange thing about the MYSTERIOUS TRACKS was that the animal appeared to only have two feet, and therefore two legs.

The only animals Oscar knew of that had two legs were …

## Bears

Like Cave Bear. But when he walked he tended to scamper about on all fours. He only reared up on his hind legs to reach food, or to make himself look big and important.

## Owls

Owl could walk around on two feet, but he didn't do it much because it was much easier to fly everywhere, and in any case his feet didn't make tracks like the ones Oscar had seen.

Which only left ...

... HUMANS!

But everybody knew Humans were more likely to eat
animals than oranges, and as Arabella said nobody
would take the idea seriously unless Oscar could
provide some PROOF.

The next day on the way to the Academy
Oscar had not given up on the idea, and at playtime
he suggested that they all play a new game called
'catch the orange thief by finding more tracks'.

At first it proved tremendously popular, but
gradually, as no more tracks were found, enthusiasm
for the game dwindled so Oscar decided to drop it.

And with no more thefts reported, interest at
the Academy had moved on to other matters.

Like inventing stand-up-wheeled-sleds.

Oscar, Arabella and all their friends enjoyed outdoor sports especially sledging. But the only problem was that if a traditional sledge hit a rock, or a bit of mud where there wasn't much snow it would stop. This is where Oscar's invention came in …

STAGE 1

FIRST OF ALL HE GOT AN OLD BIT OF WOOD AND STOOD ON IT.

STAGE 2

WHEELS ARE ADDED…

THE INVENTION MK II

Not everyone was convinced by it, especially after the rabbits crashed headfirst into a tree, but Fox remained a firm supporter. In fact, due to his enthusiasm for just about everything, Fox had quickly become Oscar's best new friend at the Academy.

Fox was also full of interesting ideas of his own.

Every afternoon after sport with Mr Strong, Mrs Mop would oversee all the animals having a good hot shower, followed by fur (or feather) drying and fur (or feather) brushing.

59

Fox was less than keen about the whole thing though.

What's the point in having to wash every day at the Academy, and then dry yourself after you've washed, and then having to brush your fur after you've dried it, and then having to do the same thing all over again when you get home? And then having to do the same thing all over again when you go to the Academy?

'But you don't wash much at home,' said Owl.

'No,' admitted Fox. 'But listen … I met this warthog in the second year the other day who said that after about two months of not washing you don't need to wash at all. Your fur just naturally starts to self-clean itself. And all of a sudden you don't smell and you don't have to wash ever again. Doesn't that sound great?'

Oscar had his doubts about Fox's great idea.

'Well anyway,' Fox continued. 'Starting from today I'm not going to clean myself at all, and then in about two months or so I'll be self-cleaning and it'll be hassle-free living.'

Fox seemed quite pleased with himself and his great idea.

Oscar wasn't convinced though. He didn't like to say it but Fox didn't smell that nice at the best of times.

The first thing that happened to Fox on his first 'stop washing ever again' day was that the caretaker accidentally poured a vat of three-day-old poo all over him that he was emptying from the Ice Age loos, but this didn't put Fox off the idea. Far from it.

'Well you see, if this had happened before, I would have been really upset because it would have taken me ages to get clean. But now I've stopped washing, I'm not bothered at all. In two months it'll all be gone and I'll be as fresh as a daisy.'

# CHAPTER 5
# HUMAN STUDIES

Oscar was beginning to really enjoy life at the Academy.

He seemed to have a particular talent for sports and Mr Strong was very pleased with Oscar's efforts on the ice lake. Arabella was good at ice skating too, and the two of them enjoyed skating fantastic routines together, much to the amusement of the rabbits and Ormsby.

After sports Mrs Mop would oversee the wool, fur and feather washing. Arabella, Prunella and the other girls would spend ages combing and plaiting their hair.

Oscar and the rest of the boys would get the whole process over with as quickly as possible, and Fox, by various means, was managing to avoid getting wet altogether.

He was also managing to miss his infrequent baths at home, and although he seemed to think his fur would become self-cleaning at any moment, everyone else had their doubts.

But the lesson that everyone enjoyed the most was HUMAN STUDIES.

'Out of all the animals in the land the one to be feared the most is of course THE HUMAN,' said Professor Snout.

'This is what a Human looks like.
Ugly-looking brute isn't he?
And this is the female of the species.

'Their cubs are called children, but don't let their size deceive you. They're probably the most tricky and dangerous of them all.'

The class shuddered.

'Now if you get your books ready we will begin ...'

# Where they live

In caves and primitive huts,

They leave tracks like these...

...and droppings like this.

And they eat YOU
all of YOU
except your wool and bone
because after they have
eaten you they'll wear
your wool and make a ~~to~~
house out of your bones.

HOME SWEET HOME

WOOLLY HAT

'Yes, Humans are the most dangerous animals in the land!' Professor Snout continued.

The whole class shuddered again.

Oscar had been thoroughly enjoying the lesson, making little notes in the margins of his exercise book and imagining what it would be like to come face to face with a real Human, when his attention was drawn to something outside the classroom. It looked like the trees had been jostled.

Oscar put down his pen and peered out of the window when all of a sudden about fifteen or twenty faces appeared at the icy glass and then quickly disappeared again. Faces EXACTLY like the ones Professor Snout had been drawing on the blackboard!

'Sir, SIRRR!' shouted Oscar with his trunk and two feet in the air.

'I've seen Humans, Sir. I've seen a whole bunch of them!'

'Yes, I know, Oscar. I've been drawing them on the blackboard for the last half an hour.'

'No, I mean I've just seen REAL HUMANS! REAL HUMANS OUTSIDE THIS CLASSROOM!!!!'

# CHAPTER 6
# TRUNK TROUBLES

But instead of sounding the special alarm gong and calling all the students to arms, all Professor Snout said was, 'Well that's impossible, Oscar. There aren't any Humans living for miles around here. And I've heard about the rumours you've been spreading about the MYSTERIOUS TRACKS and the orange thief and all the rest of it but it simply isn't possible. You probably saw a wild boar rooting in the bushes. Sometimes they come round the Academy looking for scraps. I'll put the caretaker on to it and make

sure the bins are secured properly.

'Right, as I was saying ... Humans are the most dangerous animals in all Mammothdom ...'

This was all a little too much for Oscar. That lunch break he sneaked out of the playground with Fox, Arabella and the rest of his classmates to look at the area outside the window.

There didn't seem to be any signs of Human activity about though.

Are you <u>sure</u> it wasn't a boar ...?

asked Prunella.

Perhaps it was the wind rustling the bushes...?

said Fox.

said Arabella.

chuckled Ormsby.

All that afternoon there were more heavy falls of wet slushy snow, but that didn't stop Oscar. He kept looking all lunchtime and evening playtime too.

And all the way home, and all around the herd until after dark.

He carried on looking the next morning all the way to the Academy.

By the time he got to class it was as plain as the trunk on his face that Oscar was not well.

For starters he kept sneezing.

'Hi guys how are … ATCHOOOOOOO!'

And then there was the trunk-blowing.
And the weepy eyes.
And the woolly hearing.

Poor Oscar, everyone thought. He must
have been going down with a cold, thought he'd
seen something out the window in his half-ill state,
and then good and properly gone down with the

sniffles after all this silly searching.

But Oscar would not stop. He kept searching all lunchtime, and playtime, and in between lessons, and all the way home and all around the herd until dark.

The next day in class Oscar sat at the back sniffling and looking even worse.

Even Oscar admitted that he had been over-doing things.

Arabella suggested they get him some nice soft leaves to blow his trunk on. Professor Snout said that was a good idea and gave her permission to go off to collect some. It took several hours but at last she came back with a big heap and it seemed to help.

Owl and Cave Cat thought it might be a good idea to put Oscar's feet in a bucket of hot water and so, with Professor Snout's permission, they went off to collect some snow, which they took to the kitchens for Cook to heat up. That seemed to help too.

Ormsby thought some blankets might be a good idea, so he spent a couple of hours collecting wool from around the place, which he knitted into a lovely warm blanket. This seemed to help too.

Professor Snout went out to forage for some berries to use to make some hot berry juice.

And then Oscar ran out of soft leaves to blow his trunk on so Fox and Arabella went out to collect some more.

SNIFF
SNIFF

Gradually over the week Oscar felt much better. I wish the same could be said of his classmates and teacher though.

Sniff.

Sniff.

'Atchooooo!'

Later that afternoon in the sickbay …

# CHAPTER 7
# THE MOUNTAIN TRAIL

With the cold and muddy weather and the shortage of oranges, it didn't take long for the whole Academy to go down with the sniffles. First it was all of Oscar's class and Professor Snout. Then it was Professor Bristle and his year group, until the entire Academy was ill. Even Cook was sniffling and sneezing but somehow managed to keep going, making gentle little meals of scrambled eggs and prunes for everyone.

Oscar was feeling much better though, and he had got to thinking about the Humans again. Perhaps he had been mistaken. Perhaps the faces he saw at the window had been to do with the fact he was sick. Perhaps he had imagined it all?

It had been really kind of his classmates to look after him when he was poorly. It was a shame they were all so ill now though. He decided it was the least he could do to go in search of some more berries and soft leaves to help get everyone fit again. He knew it would take more berries and leaves than he could carry to get the entire Academy better, so he took his stand-up-wheeled-sled invention to carry them back.

Oscar thought that this might also be a good opportunity to give it another test. It was a shame nobody could join him but it would enable him to fine-tune the details of the design before letting the rabbits have another go.

Oscar began climbing up into the forest to collect leaves, which he then held under his arm as he raced down the slope to put in a pile at the bottom. This was very exciting.

He began to climb further up the mountain into the trees following a little track. The extra height and the twisting bends made the descent even more thrilling. It also meant he could take the jump at the bottom a little bit faster, and fly a little bit further. 'Wheeeeeeeeee!'

Oscar decided to climb even higher up the mountain.

Then, a couple of minutes' walk up the track, he came across some footprints. They looked similar to the ones he had seen on his first day, except these ones looked fresher. There was a clearly defined outline of a foot which looked identical to the diagrams in Professor Snout's class. It was a HUMAN FOOTPRINT!

PROOF! The proof he had been looking for!

Humans here, in the valley!!

This left Oscar with a difficult choice; he could either rush back to the Academy now and tell everyone, or follow the footprints to see where they led.

But he had already told them twice that he thought Humans were sneaking about on Academy grounds! If they didn't believe him then why should they believe him now?

The footprints continued up the
mountainside, at times getting quite muddy.
Alongside the footprints Oscar had begun to notice
the odd piece of orange peel, or some banana skin,
or cherry pips. This Human had been snacking all
the way, and leaving the litter to prove it.

Oscar was beginning to feel a little nervous
and thought that perhaps it was time to turn back
when, suddenly, he was hit by the most terrible smell!
It was like dung smeared with rotten cabbage and
off-cheese, and it was so pungent it made his trunk
smart and his eyes water, but it was also vaguely
familiar.

'FOX! What on earth are you doing here?!'

'Well,' said Fox. 'With everyone being ill with colds and everything I decided to visit them in the sickbay but nobody seemed that pleased to see me and, once they heard that you had gone out to test your invention, they insisted that I go and find you. Cave Bear even gave me half his sandwich if I went, which I thought was most generous of him. Would you like a bit?'

Oscar decided not.

Fox had become even stinkier. Most of the animals at the Academy had begun to avoid him. Even Oscar tended to stand up-wind of him if possible, and always tried to open a window in his presence. But he was glad to have a friend along with him.

Slowly they trudged onwards and upwards, following the muddy trail of footprints and orange peel and discarded pips higher up the mountain, until eventually another set of footprints joined the original set of tracks.

So now there were two small Humans.

A little further on another set of tracks appeared joining the first two.

Soon more tracks appeared from the undergrowth, until it was impossible to say how many there were.

'Perhaps we ought to hop on my invention now and trundle back down the mountain to warn the others,' said Oscar.

'We could,' said Fox, 'though the higher we go up the mountain with the wheeled sled, the faster we'll come down it, so the quicker we'll get back to the Academy.

'And besides, we've come this far so we might as well carry on a tiny little bit further, even if we are scared.'

About twenty metres up the hill the forest opened out into a clearing where the tracks led right up to and into a cave.

The friends agreed that they would carefully tiptoe across the clearing, take a quick peek in the cave and then immediately turn tail and launch themselves down the mountain on the sled. Even if they did get spotted they would be able to get back to the Academy much faster than any Human could run.

Oscar and Fox nervously tiptoed up to the cave entrance and carefully peered around the corner.

# CHAPTER 8
## CAVE SKOOL

In the cave, some other young animals were having lessons. They seemed to be very excited.

Oscar and Fox crept a little further into the cave to get a better look. This is what they saw …

105

On the walls were some badly spelt bits of
writing along with primitive stick-like drawings.

# LESSON 1

WE NEEDS TO EAT FOODS OR
WE GET HUNGRY.

# FOODS WE
## EAT

THE INSIDE OF
ROUND ORANGE
THINGS

(THE OUTSIDE TASTES

HORIBLE )

THE INSIDE
OF LONG
YELLOW
THINGS

SMALL RED THINGS BUT NOT THE GREEN BIT
TASTIEST FOOD
AND THE INSIDES OF THESE BIG THINGS COOKED OVER A FIRE.

# LESSON 2

## ~~HATEI~~ CLUBS

### AND HOW TO MAKE THEM.

THIS IS A CLUB

YOU MAKE A CLUB BY GETTING A TREE, BREAKING A BIT OFF.

CRACK!!

DON'T MAKE YOUR CLUB TOO BIG

OR TOO SMALL

# THINGS PHAT CLUBS CAN BE USED FOR

① SMASHING THINGS

② HITTING THINGS

③ SCARING THINGS

AND CAPTURING
THESE BIG THINGS
SO ~~FREE~~
THEY KAN BE
COOKED OVER A
BIG HOT FIRE
AND EATEN

So the Humans *were* responsible for stealing the fruit from the Academy!

Around the cave were clubs of all different shapes and sizes. It didn't take Oscar and Fox long to work out what was about to happen next.

Not only had a tribe of Humans set up a cave school in the mammoth lands, and not only were they stealing oranges and now bananas and cherries from the kitchens, but it seemed now they were planning a hunting trip to get some FRESH MEAT leaving that very afternoon! The Academy must be warned AT ONCE!

Oscar and Fox turned around and began to edge back out of the cave. But Fox wasn't feeling well. He was feeling a little bit sneezy.

'Ahhhh

'Ahhhhhhh … ATCHOOOOOOOOOO!'

Standing in the cave entrance was a huge, enormous Human waving his fists and growling. He seemed very upset.

'UGH!

'UGHHHHHHH!

'UGHHHHHHHHHHHHHHHHHHHHHH!'

He picked up the wheeled-sled invention ...

... and CRASH he bashed it down into the ground, splintering it in two. He started advancing towards them still clutching half the sled in his fist.

# CHAPTER 9
# TRAPPED!

By now the rest of the cave school had spotted them too.

'Ugh. Ugh. UGH!'

Professor Ugh started grunting orders at his pupils and they began to form a ring around Oscar and Fox, forcing them back into the cave.

'Are they going to bash us with clubs and eat us?' whispered Fox, nervously.

'No,' replied Oscar. 'I think it's worse than that. I think they're going to keep us here whilst the rest of them attack the Academy and eat our friends and teachers, and then they're going to come back here and bash us with clubs and eat us for dessert.'

'Crumbs,' said Fox.

Oscar and Fox looked on helplessly whilst the rest of the Humans went to pick up their clubs and organize themselves into a hunting pack.

All seemed to be going to plan, apart from one Human who was having a problem picking up his club. This was probably because it was at least seven and a half times the size of him. Eventually he picked up a twig and went to join the others.

'UGH, UGH, UGH, UGH.'

'UGH, UGH, UGH, UGH.'

'UGH, UGH, UGH, UGH.'

The hunting party began marching off down the mountain towards the Academy.

Meanwhile the huge, enormous Human was left to guard Oscar and Fox.

Oscar and Fox sat down in despair, desperately looking for a way out.

In the middle of the cave was a huge roaring fire. Oscar thought that the Humans must need it to keep warm, as they seemed to have much thinner coats than either of them. It was causing Oscar and Fox to get a little hot and sweaty.

Imagine if you were covered from head to toe in two layers of thick wool. A hot, stuffy, airless cave is the last place you'd want to be. In fact, because they were nervous and upset and worried, they were sweating much more than normal. And now, in this confined space Fox was beginning to get very stinky indeed. In fact, it was almost becoming a little bit too much for Oscar to bear.

He pinched his trunk shut and tried to think of nice things like flowers and the smell behind Arabella's ears. The huge, enormous Human guarding them seemed to be having an even harder time. He was holding his nose too and trying to hold his breath, every now and then having to gulp down a sniff of the toxic air that would make his eyes bulge and cause him to clutch his throat and shudder.

And then Oscar had an idea.

A ONE, TWO...
A ONE, TWO...

HANDSTANDS.

ONE, TWO. ONE, TWO.
ONE, TWO!

WAVE THOSE ARMPITS!

HEY FOX, WHISPERED OSCAR. IF YOU NEED TO FART...

... NOW IS THE TIME TO DO IT!!

PARPPPPPP!!

This proved too much for their guard, who ran scrabbling out of the cave yowling like a scalded cat, before fainting to the ground with an almighty THUDDD!

Now was their chance.

Oscar and Fox ran out of the cave after him, but by now the hunting trip was long gone. Even if they ran their fastest they would never get to the Academy in time to warn them.

There was only one thing to do …

It was no wonder the stupid Human had been unable to lift the giant club. Even Oscar and Fox together found it hard to heave it even a few inches off the ground, but eventually the four wheels that had previously been attached to Oscar's stand-up-wheeled-sled invention were now firmly attached to the bottom.

It took a while to get it moving, but once it got going it seemed to pick up speed surprisingly quickly …

'WOOOOOOOO!'
'WHEEEEEEEE!'
'Aghhhhh!'

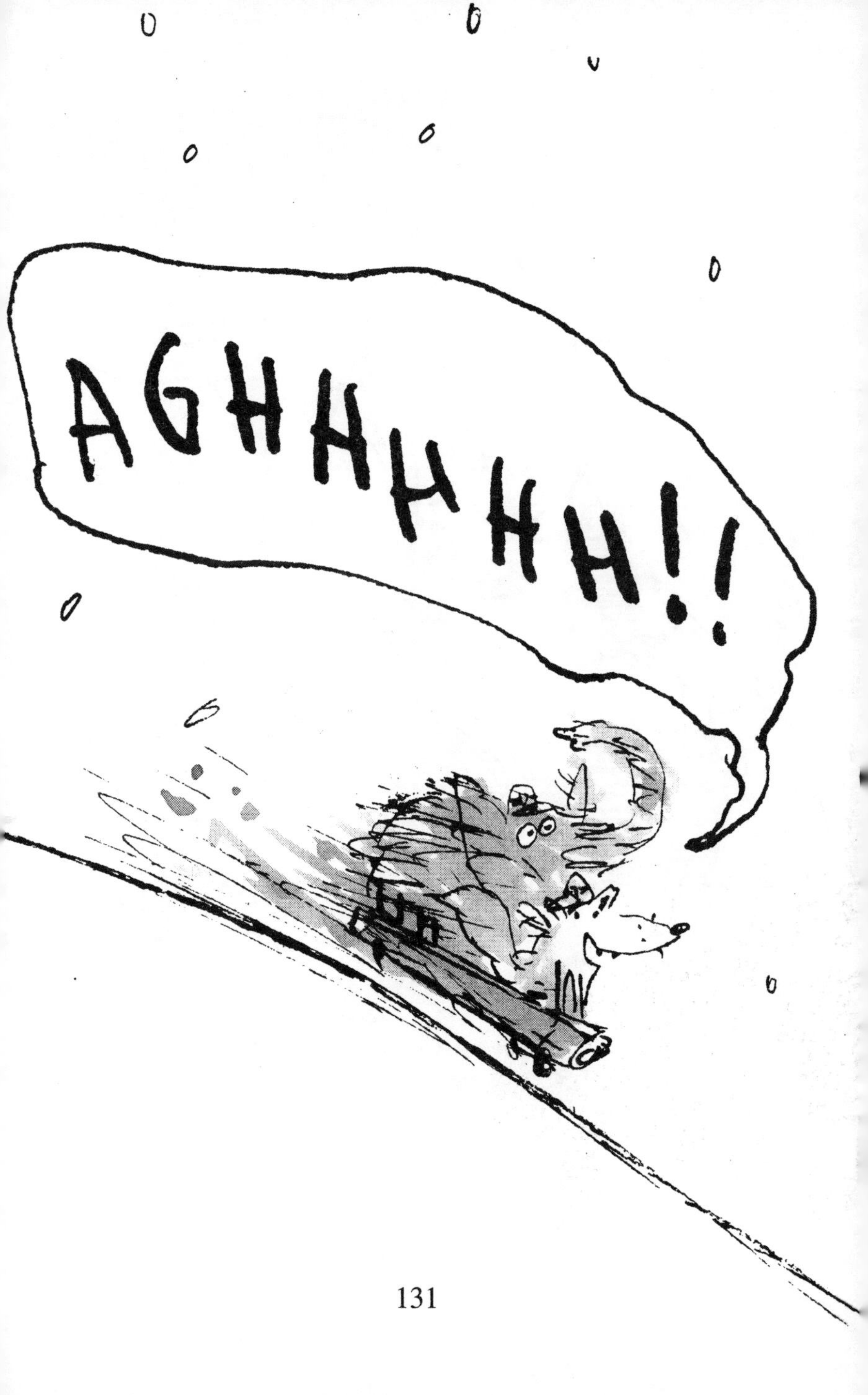
AGHHHHH!!

# CHAPTER 10
# CRASHHH!

This was quite possibly the best thing Oscar or Fox had ever done in their lives. The invention was now travelling at breakneck speed down the mountainside, spraying slush and mud and the occasional bit of Human dung all over its riders. Every now and then they would hit a little bump and go flying high above the treetops before coming crashing down again through snow-laden bushes and branches. They were totally covered in leaves and grass, sopping wet with snow and mud, and gaining momentum all the time.

CRASH!

'Yeeeeaaaaahhhh!'

To turn, Oscar or Fox had to shout 'LEFT!' or 'RIGHT!' and then they would both lean over as far as they could. 'Wooooooo!'

'UGH, UGH, UGH, UGH!'

The Humans' hunting party continued its march down the mountainside towards the Academy.

The first they knew of Oscar and Fox's pursuit was the sound of trees and bushes being uprooted higher up the mountain. Then the smell of Fox hit them.

And suddenly CRASH it burst into view. The biggest, smelliest, scariest, noisiest, fastest mud-covered four-eyed monster they had ever seen.

The Humans turned to flee from its approach.

'UGHHHH! UGHHHHHHHHHHHHH! UGGH!'

Oscar and Fox were amazed at how fast Humans could run if they needed to. 'You wouldn't have thought their little legs could go round that quickly,' observed Oscar.

They had by now emerged from the forest and were herding the Humans directly towards the cliff and the marshy marsh.

'Erm, what happens when we get to the cliff?' asked Fox. But Oscar didn't have time to answer.

The Humans got to the edge of the cliff first. Most of them were going so quickly they didn't have time to stop and they just plopped straight over the edge. The others decided they would rather jump off a forty-foot cliff into a frozen marsh than face the hideous, smelly, scary, giant, speeding monster bearing down on them.

Oscar and Fox hit the edge of the cliff considerably faster than any of the Humans.

'Wooooooooooo!'

As they were catapulted high up into the air, the Humans far below them flailed waist-deep in the icy mud, covering their eyes and moaning in fear.

'Aggghhhhhh!'

Oscar and Fox had never flown before, and certainly not this high and in these circumstances. They found the sensation most agreeable.

Amazingly, they seemed to be flying over the entire marshy marsh and heading towards …

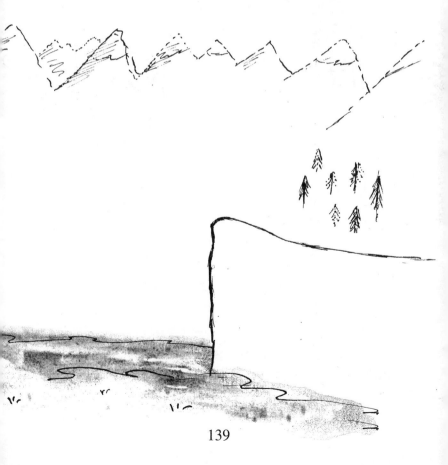

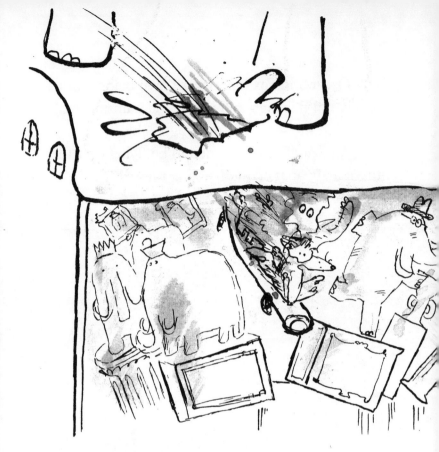

... the Academy. CRASSHHHHHH!!!

They hit the ancient ice roof first, and then smashed through at least two floors of empty storage space, before finally emerging through the ancient arched ceiling of the Great Hall of Mammoth Sculptures.

Professor Snout, who had been in the sculpture hall at the time, was for a second or two, completely speechless.

But once he had realized what was happening, he snapped into action.

BONG! BONG! BONG! The special alarm-gong was sounded.

All those animals who weren't completely bedridden with sniffles were immediately called up to defend the walls of the Academy.

A second party of mammoths was sent out to as hurl as many snowballs as mammothly possible down into the marsh to drive the Humans back up into the forest.

The Humans, already panicky and fearful and covered from head to toe in snow and marshy marsh mud, did not need much encouragement to turn tail and flee as fast as they could.

That evening a special meeting was called where the whole Academy was brought up to speed with events.

Oscar and Fox were commended for saving the Academy.

And everyone else was praised for snapping to attention and being really good at making tons of snowballs.

And although the headmistress mammoth warned everybody to be on the lookout for Humans, it was agreed that a celebration was called for and a special feast was declared to celebrate their victory.

Cook baked a special cake for the occasion – and managed to find some more oranges and cherries to serve up with it, to make sure that everybody got their daily ration of fruit and nobody got the sniffles again.

Oscar and Fox were heralded as guests of honour, and Fox surprised everyone by taking a shower beforehand.

In fact, Arabella and Prunella hardly recognized him when they presented the brave friends with bunches of flowers.

The rabbits performed some special music whilst Cave Bear and Owl sang a special song, and Ormsby and Giant Sloth performed a special dance.

Everyone joined in the party and ate – LOTS!
It was mammoth-tastic!

# CHAPTER 11
# FINALLY!

For the rest of term all lessons were cancelled and the pupils instead spent their time re-building the Academy – which, with so many helping paws and trunks, didn't take long. There was no more trouble from the Humans – who were probably still recovering from shock.

And forever after, one day each year, all the animals were allowed to get as SMELLY as possible.

Nobody ever beat Fox though.

He really was the stinkiest.

*Another mammoth adventure from Smarties Award winner Neal Layton*

# Oscar and Arabella and ORMSBY

OSCAR AND ARABELLA ARE THE BEST OF FRIENDS.

And then ORMSBY

appears on the scene.

You know what they say: 'Two's company and three's a crowd!'

A terrific book about making new friends.

"... an eclectic mix of scribbles, prints and hilarious facial expressions ..."

*Another tale from Smarties Award winner*
*Neal Layton*

# THE STORY OF EVERYTHING

## BY NEAL LAYTON

Once upon a very long time ago there was nothing.

No space, no time, no planets, no people, no me, no you, no nothing, until...

An ingenious novelty book about evolution.
It will literally BLOW YOU AWAY!

*Another story from Smarties Award winner*
*Neal Layton*

# BARTHOLOMEW

## and the B U G

By Neal Layton

Bartholomew is used to a quiet life and
he likes to take things nice and easy.
Then one day a crazy bug turns
up who is in a terribly tremendous
hurry to find the bright lights. So being
the kindly bear that he is, Bartholomew
decides to help him get to the
big **bright city** .

A refreshing, original tale
about morality.

## Steve's Sunday Blues
### Neal Layton

What is good about Sundays?

Walking the dog, splashing in puddles,
visiting Auntie Vera and yummeroony food!

So why has Steve got the Sunday Blues?

Could it be because Monday Morning is just
around the corner …

This hilarious picture book will delight anyone who
has ever dreaded Monday Morning!

## Stinky Finger's House of Fun
## Jon Blake

The Spoonheads have arrived in their space-hoovers
and sucked up all the grown-ups! So Stinky and Icky
will never have to change their underwear again.

In search of an Aim in Life, the two great mates
head off to Uncle Nero's House of Fun.
But soon they're being besieged by an army of pigs
who want to make people pies!

They're going to need more than Icky's lucky
feather and Stinky's smelly pants to
save their crazy new home …

## The Magician's Boy
## Susan Cooper

Once upon a time there was a
Boy who worked for a Magician.
He polished the Magician's wands and caught
the rabbits that the Magician pulled out of hats.
But what he wanted most of all
was to learn magic himself.

Follow the Boy as he is transported to the
Land of Story on a magical quest.
Adventure and familiar characters are
at every turn and a perfect ending awaits…

**'Perfect for reading aloud, the tale will
encourage readers and listeners to revisit
familiar fairy tales and nursery rhymes.'**
**KIRKUS REVIEWS**

## Books for Boys
## Ian Whybrow, illustrated by Tony Ross

Ever wished you had super powers? What about being a racing-car driver? Or a knight? Or the star player of your school football team?

Have you ever broken your mum's favourite vase? Or got stuck in the cat-flap?

Read about adventures just like the ones you've had or ones you've dreamed you could have.

In this hilarious ten-book series, there's certainly something for everyone! Even the boy who had (nearly) everything …